GALLOWS HILL

and

The Ghostly Penny

MARTIN WADDELL

Illustrated by JAMES MAYHEW

ORCHARD BOOKS

For Max, with love

J.M

ORCHARD BOOKS
96 Leonard Street, London EC2A 4XD
Hachette Children's Books Australia
Level 17/207 Kent Street, Sydney NSW 2000
ISBN 1 84362 427 3 (hardback)
ISBN 1 84362 432 X (paperback)
The text was first published in the form
of a gift collection called *The Orchard Book of Ghostly Stories*
illustrated by Sophy Williams, in Great Britain in 2000
This edition first published in hardback in 2005
First paperback publication in 2006
The Orchard Book of Ghostly Stories
Text © Martin Waddell 2000
Illustrations © James Mayhew 2005
The rights of Martin Waddell to be identified as the author
and of James Mayhew to be identified as the illustrator of this work
have been asserted by them in accordance with the
Copyright, Designs and Patents Act, 1988.
A CIP catalogue record for this book is available
from the British Library.
1 3 5 7 9 10 8 6 4 2 (hardback)
1 3 5 7 9 10 8 6 4 2 (paperback)
Printed in Great Britain
www.wattspublishing.co.uk

CONTENTS

GALLOWS HILL

One night Sam Bonny was coming home on the old donkey he had bought at the fair with the money he got for selling his eggs. He had stayed on at the fair after buying the donkey, and so it was dusk when he came to the crossroad at Strule, on his way to his house on the slopes of Slieve Crobe, in the townland of Menagh.

As everyone knows, there are two
roads that go from Strule on to Menagh.

One road leads by the black bog into
Menagh. It is the long road, and it's
muddy. The short road is the road by
the hill with the gallows. No one goes
by that road in the dark, but Sam Bonny
did.

He wanted to get
to his home before
dawn, and Strule
is a long way from
Menagh if you take
the bog road, but
no distance at all if
you go by the hill.

There was always
some poor body
hung out
on the hill.

As everyone knows, men don't take that road because of the corpses that hang out on the hill.

"Well, so there it is!" Sam told himself. "But what corpse would be bothering me? If I go by the hill I'll be home before dawn, and if I go by the Bog I'll be covered in mud and home late."

He'd a day's work to do on the farm the next day, and so he set off on the road to the hill.

He had no bother till he came to the gallows.

His neighbour Jackie Golightly swung there, strung up and choked for poaching a salmon belonging to the magistrate, Big Lord McGill.

As everyone knows, Big Lord McGill is a keen fisherman, and likes to catch his own salmon.

Everyone knew, and Jackie Golightly didn't mean to be caught, but he was, and so he was sentenced and hanged, for the salmon.

The donkey stopped there, at the gallows, and it laid its ears back and brayed, looking up at the corpse of Jackie Golightly. "God rest your soul!" Sam said. He crossed himself thrice, to ward off the curse, and he tipped his hat to the corpse, for there's no harm in being polite. "It's a hard thing to be hanged for eating a fish."

Everyone knows Sam didn't eat fish, except on a Friday, when his wife made him eat fish and like it.

Then Sam tapped the donkey to make it go on.

The donkey wouldn't move!

That's when Sam remembered why the donkey had been cheap at the fair. It had belonged to Jackie Golightly before he was hanged! Jackie's things had been sold at the fair to pay up the debts that he owed, and repay Big Lord McGill for his salmon.

"You belong to me now," he told the donkey. "For you are no use to Jackie Golightly, up there."

The donkey wouldn't see sense.

Sam got off and pulled, but the donkey pulled back. It wasn't leaving Jackie Golightly.

Sam sat down and thought at the foot of the gallows, with Jackie Golightly swinging above him.

"If the beast won't go on, maybe it will go back," Sam thought, so he pulled the donkey the other way, back down the way leading to Strule.

The donkey stuck its hoofs in and stayed where it was, under the legs of Jackie Golightly.

"You won't come, you won't go!" Sam scolded the donkey.

The donkey stood placid and still. It was waiting for Jackie Golightly to tell it to come or to go.

"We're not staying here," Sam told the donkey. "I paid my good egg-money so I could ride, and we're not staying here on this hill."

11

The donkey sat down. It
wouldn't go without
Jackie Golightly.
It wouldn't go, and Sam
wouldn't leave it, but
somehow he had to get
home before dawn,
and with him he
wanted the donkey to
prove how he'd spent
the egg-money. His wife was the
kind who might say he had spent the
egg-money on drink if he went home,

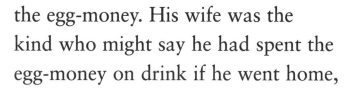

leaving the donkey behind.
"Talk sense, donkey
dear," Sam said
to the donkey.
As everyone knows,
there's no talking
sense to a donkey.

There was only one thing to be done, and Sam did it, for he wasn't leaving his newly-bought donkey for Jackie Golightly to keep.

He got out his knife, and he climbed up the gallows and cut down the corpse of Jackie Golightly.

"We'll take Jackie with us," Sam told the donkey, and he loaded Jackie up on its back.

That pleased the donkey.

It pleased the donkey, but it didn't please Sam because Jackie Golightly was riding the beast, and Sam was left walking beside them, trying to hold Jackie's corpse in its place. Jackie Golightly kept slipping and sliding about on the back of the beast, for Jackie was dead and he couldn't hang on to the donkey.

"There's room for one more on your back," Sam told the donkey and he climbed up behind Jackie Golightly, wrapping his arm round the corpse to hold it on as they rode.

They went down Gallows Hill, the donkey, and Sam, and the dead man, jogging along at the slow pace of the donkey.

Sam was pleased with himself for solving the problem.

"Never mind, Jackie," said Sam. "This is better than walking!"

If the corpse nodded its head, it must have been that its poor neck was broken.

As everyone knows, no corpse can go nodding its head, especially a corpse that's been dead for a week, and hung out in the cold.

The trouble started halfway to Menagh, and halfway to Sam's home. They were drawing close to the lane leading up to the house that belonged to Jackie Golightly, before he was hanged.

Sam had his hand on the rein that he'd rigged, an old bit of rope that he used for a belt for his trousers. He'd brought no rein with him when he went to the fair, for he hadn't thought he'd be coming home with a donkey. Donkeys came dear, but this one had come cheap, because it had belonged to Jackie Golightly.

As everyone knows, a dead man's donkey doesn't bring luck with the stripe on its back, and there hadn't been many bidders.

Sam had his hand on the rope, holding it loose, for the donkey knew the road well. He'd been down it before, with Jackie Golightly.

Sam had one hand round the waist of the corpse that was riding before him, and one hand on the rope.

Then the corpse moved.

It put out its hand, and tugged on the rope, at least Sam thought it did (although Sam knew it couldn't). And the donkey thought it did too. At least that's how Sam explains why the donkey turned up the lane at Golightly's.

18

"Whoa there, donkey!" cried Sam, but the donkey went on up the lane, making light of the weight on its back, that was Jackie Golightly, and Sam.

They rode into the yard at Golightly's.

The donkey came to a stop by the door, for it knew its journey was done, and it wanted a bag and some feed.

As everyone knows, a donkey deserves its desserts.

"Well, this is a to-do!" muttered Sam.

The corpse nodded again, or Sam thought it did.

Sam cursed the donkey, and got off its back.

The corpse climbed off too, all by itself.

"Back home again!" said the corpse, with a sigh, rubbing its hand on the weals round its neck.

As everyone knows, corpses don't sigh when they've been dead a week, but this corpse did, greatly upsetting poor Sam.

"You'd best be on your way," said the corpse. "For this is my home and your home's over there, Sammy Bonny."

Sam was upset, but he wasn't leaving the donkey he'd bought fair and square at the fair, at the cost of his hard-earned egg-money.

"It may be your home," Sam said, "but the donkey is mine, for I bid a good price at the fair!"

"You bought a cheap ride that would carry you home," said the corpse. "Now you've had a ride that was worth every penny you paid. You've had your ride, Sammy, and I'm having my donkey!"

"The donkey is mine!" Sam said, standing up for his rights, although he was quaking inside. "This donkey is mine, 'cause you're dead."

"Dead I may be," said the corpse. "But I'm not staying here. I'm moving along on my donkey, in case they might swing me again on the gallows. For Gallows Hill is a cold place, and lonely, when you're hanging about and can't even hear your heart beat."

"I'm sorry you're dead," Sam said. "But I paid my egg-money, and I need the cash, or the donkey."

That seemed to make the corpse mad.

"What's your egg-money to me now I'm dead?" said the corpse, and it reached out for Sam and fixed its cold hands round Sam's throat.

That was too much
for Sam Bonny.

The corpse wasn't
strong (it had, after
all, been dead for a
week, and was just
a bit into decay) so
Sam shook it off, and
he ran down the lane
and away up the road.

That's how Sam explained coming
home from the fair with no donkey
to show for his money.

"It's lies! You
spent our
egg-money on
drink!" Sam's wife
cried, and she
didn't feed him
for a week.

Everyone knew she was right.

Everyone knew…but…

Why was there no corpse on the gallows the next day? Corpses don't just ride away, and everyone knows Jackie Golightly was deader than dead for a week, stiff as a board and well into decay.

Well, everyone knew, but the donkey.

THE GHOSTLY PENNY

This story is as much about a place as it is about people, for people are made by the places they live in, like the cold lonely mountain at Creevy.

Abe and Marty Quinn lived there. They were brothers, but they had a grudge between them over a penny they'd lost, when their mother had sent them for milk a long time ago.

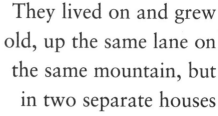 They lived on and grew
old, up the same lane on
the same mountain, but
in two separate houses
living alone, and all for the
sake of a greasy old penny for milk.

One day Abe took a cold in the chest,
and the next day he was dead.

If Marty was sad that his brother had
died, he didn't show it.

He went to the graveside when his
brother was buried, and spoke never a
word. He dropped the last sod on the lid
of the coffin, then he went to wait for
the bus to go home.

Abe's ghost was waiting for him at the bus stop, and it had a strange look on its face, as though it was fretting.

The Ghost didn't speak, but neither did Marty.

The old man and the Ghost sat on the window-ledge of Higgins' Shoe Shop, waiting for the bus to come round the Square.

The bus came, and Marty got on.

"I was sorry to hear about your brother," the driver said to Marty.

"There was no love lost between us," Marty said.

He didn't care if the Ghost heard him.

The Ghost got on the bus after Marty, but the driver didn't speak to him or punch his ticket. It was as if the Ghost wasn't there.

The Ghost came down the aisle of the bus, and sat in the seat behind his brother.

There were two young girls sitting opposite the Ghost, but they didn't see him.

There's only me can see him! Marty thought.

Marty got off at the crossroads. So did the Ghost.

They both walked
down the road to
the Mass rock, and
then they turned up
the lane towards the
Hunger fields, and the
two cottages a mile apart
on the side of the mountain.

They started up the lane, but not together.

Marty was in front, with the Ghost behind him.

It was getting dark, and the lane was still and full of shadows.

"Marty?" said the Ghost suddenly.

Marty ignored him.

"Marty?" called the Ghost a second time.

Marty stopped.

The Ghost came up beside him.

"I don't know what it is, Marty," the Ghost said. "But I feel a bit odd."

Marty said nothing. Abe being a ghost made no difference to Marty. Why should it?

The two of them, the old man and his brother's ghost, walked on up the lane without saying anything.

"Marty?" said the Ghost.

"Did you speak to me?" Marty said.

"I did," said the Ghost.

"Mind it was you who spoke first!" Marty said.

"I've something for you," said the Ghost, and he held out a penny.

Marty looked at the penny in the Ghost's hand. It looked a bit *ghostly*, and not like the kind he could cash.

"Keep your money!" he said. "It's no use to me now."

"I'm saying that I got it wrong," said the Ghost.

"If you're saying that, what are you *after*?" said Marty. He thought there must be a catch for Abe to give in just like that.

"Maybe you'd let me come indoors a minute?" suggested the Ghost.

"It would be the first time in fifty years!" said Marty.

"It would," said the Ghost.

"Well, come in if you have to," said Marty.

35

Marty went into the cottage, and the Ghost came after him. The Ghost settled in their father's old chair by the fire, where Abe used to sit before they had the quarrel.

Marty lit the oil lamp, and stirred up the fire. He threw another sod of turf on, and the glow of the flames sent a shadow dancing round the room.

Marty's shadow, that is.

The Ghost cast no shadow, although he looked solid enough.

Marty lit his pipe, and the Ghost lit his pipe.

The pair of them sat there in the firelight, and neither of them said a word.

The only sound was the ticking of their mother's wall clock.

Tick-tock, tick-tock.

A long time went by.

They sat on, puffing their pipes and not looking at each other.

They were both used to being alone. Neither of them knew what to do when it came to having company round the fire at night.

Tick-tock, tick-tock, went the clock on the wall.

"You'll be going to your bed soon," the Ghost said at last.

"There's no hurry," Marty said.

"I should be going on up the lane to my own house," the Ghost said.

Marty didn't say anything. He just sat there puffing his pipe.

The Ghost coughed and tapped his pipe against the fire and began to fidget a little bit, as if there was something on his mind.

Marty let him fidget.

"Would you mind me asking you something, Marty?" the Ghost said, clearing his throat awkwardly to say it.

"Ask on," said Marty.

"Well, I will," said the Ghost. "I was wondering, would I be, could I be…?" And he stopped, as if there was something he couldn't bring himself to say.

"Dead?" said Marty.

"Yes," said the Ghost. "That's it. Could I be dead and not know it?"

"I'd never have let you in here if you were living!" Marty said, remembering it was the brother he'd quarrelled with that he was talking to.

"I thought I was dead, only I didn't know for sure," the Ghost said.

"Well, you know now," said Marty.

They sat a bit more.

Marty put some more turf on the fire, for the glow was getting dim.

Tick-tock, tick-tock, went their mother's old clock.

"Marty?" said the Ghost.

"Yes?" said Marty.

"Marty, is there...is there a bit less of me than there was?"

Marty peered at
the Ghost. He
could see the
shape of the
chair through
the shape of his brother.

"You're a bit faded, maybe," he said.

"Oh dear," said the Ghost.

"It would be being dead that does it,"
said Marty. "You're fading away."

They sat a while longer.

Tick-tock, tick-tock.

"Am I still fading?" the Ghost asked.

"A bit more than
you were before,"
Marty said.

"I'll soon be
all gone then,"
the Ghost said.

"I suppose so, Abe," said Marty.

"You'll be wanting to go to bed," said the Ghost.

"There's no hurry," Marty said.

The fire burned low, and at last the oil lamp started to flicker, and went out.

Tick-tock, tick-tock.

"Are you there, Abe?" Marty asked.

"Aye," said the Ghost, though his voice sounded further away.

"I see you are," said Marty, peering at the figure sitting opposite him, which was now little more than a shadow in the chair.

"I'll be gone altogether, soon," said the Ghost.

"I think you will," Marty agreed.

"You are good, keeping me company, considering we never talked much all these years," said the Ghost.

"Yes," said Marty. "All over nothing, too."

"So it was," said the Ghost. "All over nothing at all."

Tick-tock, tick-tock.

They sat on. The fire burned lower and lower, down to the last few embers that glowed in the hearth.

43

"Abe?" said Marty.

Tick-tock, tick-tock.

"Are you still there, Abe?"

Tick-tock, tick-tock.

Marty peered at the chair across the fire from him.

It was empty. Nothing. Not even the ghostly old penny.

"Ah well," said Marty.

Tick-tock, tick-tock.

Marty stood up, knocked his pipe against the mantel, and went to bed. It was well past his bedtime, but of course he didn't often have company to talk to.

That left the old clock tick-tocking away all to itself in the room.

Tick-tock, tick-tock.

More about the Stories...

These stories are all my own work, but they are meant to sound and feel like the stories told by a Seancaiti, the gaelic word for a storyteller.

Imagine the loneliness of a tiny cottage on a bog road, the pitch darkness outside, the firelight and the smells of the turf. There were hidden meanings in the old stories, for those who had learned how to listen!

Martin Waddell

GALLOWS HILL

The county town near me, Downpatrick, has its own Gallows Hill up beyond Saul Street. Only the name remains, but it is a reminder of what used to be, when corpses were hung out as warning to the peasantry. I took that idea, and the idea of the drunkard's excuse when he comes home from the fair with no money, and tied them together with the tale of Jackie Golightly's donkey that wants to go home with his master. The problem is, Jackie Golightly's been hanged, and the corpse has got just a bit into decay...

THE GHOSTLY PENNY

Near where I live is a cold, grey lough called Lough Island Reavy. It is a stark, exposed stretch of water in a barren lowland place, with mountains rising from it. There are stone walls and whins and one or two little cottages and the traces of Hunger fields and an ancient underground souterrain. I was scared of the lough as a child, and I am none too comfy there as an adult. This story came from the strange feeling of that place, though somewhere along the way the lough itself got lost. I wanted to write about the remoteness of the existence of the people who lived there when I was a child, and the way a grudge could linger down the decades. It is a story about clinging on to life, in more ways than one...

Tales of Ghostly Ghouls and Haunting Horrors!

"Every story creates that sense of uneasiness which is experienced when a door creaks or a window rattles." *Carousel*

Written by Martin Waddell
Illustrated by James Mayhew

SOFT BUTTER'S GHOST
and Himself   *ISBN 1 84362 430 3*

BONELESS AND THE TINKER
and Dancing with Francie   *ISBN 1 84362 431 1*

GALLOWS HILL
and The Ghostly Penny   *ISBN 1 84362 432 X*

DEATH AND THE NEIGHBOURS AT NESS
and Little Bridget   *ISBN 1 84362 433 8*

All at £3.99

Orchard Myths are available from all good bookshops,
or can be ordered direct from the publisher:
Orchard Books, PO BOX 29, Douglas IM99 1BQ
Credit card orders please telephone 01624 836000
or fax 01624 837033
or e-mail: bookshop@enterprise.net for details.

To order please quote title, author and ISBN
and your full name and address.
Cheques and postal orders should be
made payable to 'Bookpost plc'.
Postage and packing is FREE within the UK
(overseas customers should add £1.00 per book).

Prices and availability are subject to change.